Colors! ¡Colores!

Jorge Luján
& Piet Grobler

Translated by / Traducción de
John Oliver Simon & Rebecca Parfitt

Groundwood Books / Libros Tigrillo
House of Anansi Press
Toronto   Berkeley

Rocked
by the tide,
beige
fell asleep on the sand.

El beige
se durmió en la arena
de tanto que lo arrulla
la marea.

Blue.
It's all in the sky,
except for those flowers
and that little girl's eyes.

El **azul**
está todo arriba,
salvo en unas flores
y en los ojos de una niña.

The color **pink**,
bright as a little girl's nose,
makes everything
smell like a rose.

El color **rosa**,
lo mismo que las rosas,
perfuma
hasta las más pequeñas cosas.

Yellow
rolls
through
the
sky
like
a
warm
gold
coin.

El
amarillo
rueda
por
el
cielo
como
una
moneda
de
oro
tibio.

Into a tiny seed
fits clover, fits a tree,
fits the whole jungle…
fits **green**.

En una pequeña semilla
cabe todo el **verde**,
cabe el trébol, cabe la ceiba,
cabe la selva entera.

Orange,
little sun of the orchard,
they will say I ate you,
and it's true.

Ay, naranja,
pequeño sol del huerto,
dirán que te he comido
y será cierto.

Burning spark
lands on the elm.
   Who's singing?
Red.

Una brasa encendida
se posa sobre el olmo.
   ¿Quién canta?
El **rojo**.

Brown.
A coconut floating down,
a rock far from town
where an antelope is watching.

El marrón
es un coco a la deriva,
o una roca
con un antílope encima.

I saw a lake.
I saw a flower.
I saw the twilight.
… **Violet**!

Vio un lago,
vio una flor,
vio el ocaso,
¡**violeta**!

Night has put on
her **black** gown,
so the eyes of the universe
can shine more brightly.

La noche se ha puesto
su vestido **negro**
para que luzcan más bellos
los ojos del universo.

The moon
opens and closes her fan
so slowly:
white, almost white.

Abre y cierra su abanico
la luna muy despacito:
blanco,
blanquito.

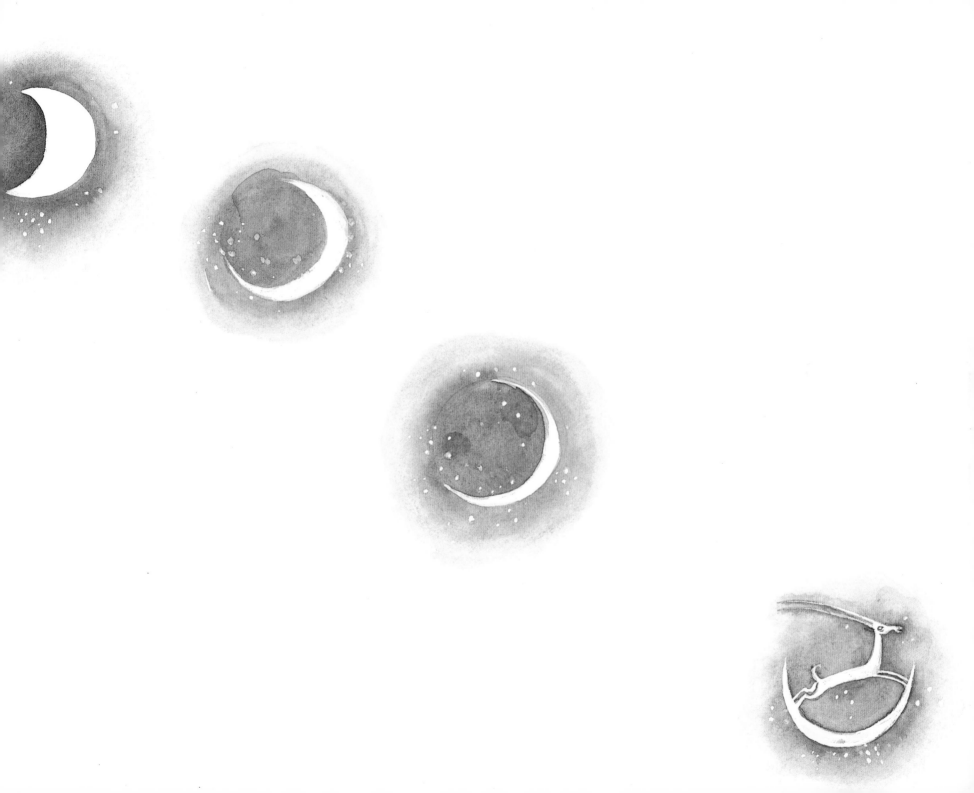

Text copyright © 2008 by Jorge Luján
Illustrations copyright © 2008 by Piet Grobler
English translation copyright © 2008 by John Oliver Simon and Rebecca Parfitt
Fourth printing 2012

Groundwood Books / House of Anansi Press
110 Spadina Avenue, Suite 801, Toronto, Ontario M5V 2K4
or c/o Publishers Group West
1700 Fourth Street, Berkeley, CA 94710

Library and Archives Canada Cataloguing in Publication
Luján, Jorge
Colors! / Jorge Luján ; illustrations by Piet Grobler ; translated by
John Oliver Simon and Rebecca Parfitt = ¡Colores! / Jorge
Luján ; ilustraciones de Piet Grobler ; traducción John Oliver
Simon and Rebecca Parfitt.
Text in English and Spanish.
ISBN 978-0-88899-863-7
1. Color–Juvenile poetry. 2. Children's poetry, Spanish American.
3. Children's poetry, English. I. Grobler, Piet II. Simon,
John Oliver III. Parfitt, Rebecca Rowe IV. Title. V. Title: ¡Colores!.
PZ73.L85Co 2008   j861'.7   C2007-904812-9

Printed and bound in China

To Didí and Mónica, for the joy
we share.

Para Didí y Mónica, por la alegría
de los días compartidos.

– JL

In memory of Adriaan, who knew
so much about color.

En memoria de Adriaan, que tanto
sabía sobre el color.

– PG